The Adventures *of* Laura & Jack

THE LITTLE HOUSE BOOKS

By Laura Ingalls Wilder

Illustrated by Garth Williams

A LITTLE HOUSE CHAPTER BOOK

LITTLE HOUSE

Laura Ingalls Wilder

The
Adventures of
Laura & Jack

LAURA INGALLS WILDER

illustrated by
RENÉE GRAEF

SCHOLASTIC INC.
New York Toronto London Auckland Sydney

Adaptation by Melissa Peterson.

ISBN 0-590-25414-6

Text adapted from *Little House in the Big Woods*,
copyright 1932, copyright renewed 1959, Roger Lea MacBride.
Illustrations copyright © 1997 by Renée Graef. All rights reserved.
Published by Scholastic Inc., 555 Broadway, New York, NY 10012,
by arrangement with HarperTrophy, a division of HarperCollins
Children's Books, a division of HarperCollins Publishers.
Little House® is a trademark of HarperCollins Publishers Inc.
SCHOLASTIC and associated logos are trademarks and/or
registered trademarks of Scholastic Inc.

12 11 10 9   9/9 0 1 2 3/0

Printed in the U.S.A.   40

First Scholastic printing, February 1998

Contents

CHAPTER 1

Laura and Jack

As far back as Laura could remember, Jack was there. When Laura and Mary, Ma and Pa, and baby Carrie lived in the Big Woods of Wisconsin, they never had to worry about the bears and wildcats that roamed the forest. Jack stood guard every night. He was a watchdog, and it was his job to keep the family safe.

Jack was a bulldog. He had a stocky body and short legs. His light-brown fur was short, with darker-brown streaks through it. He had a large head and strong, square jaws. When he was guarding the family, he looked very stern and fierce. But with Laura and Mary he was always gentle.

Laura was a very little girl in those days. Mary was a bit older, and she was quiet and good. Laura liked to run and play with Jack. There were no other children living nearby—there wasn't even another house in sight. Just trees and more trees. Laura and Jack weren't allowed to stray into the woods, but there was lots to do right around the little house. Especially if you were a dog.

In the summer Jack had squirrels to chase and birds to bark at. At night he protected Ma's garden from the deer that lived in the woods. The garden was planted behind the cabin. During the day the deer wouldn't come so close to the house, but at night they got brave and jumped the fence. If it hadn't been for Jack, they would have eaten all Ma's carrots and cabbages. Jack ran after them and chased them out. In the morning Laura would find little hoofprints among the turnips, with Jack's pawprints right beside them.

In the fall Ma and Pa were busy storing food for the winter. They gathered the turnips and cabbages and beets and piled them in the cellar. Ma braided onions into long ropes and hung them in the attic above heaps of pumpkins and squash. Pa brought deer meat home to be smoked and salted. And when the weather was just right, he butchered a pig.

Butchering time was great fun for Laura, Mary, and Jack. Pa let the girls roast the pig's tail on a stick. It sizzled and gave off a delicious smell. When it was brown all over, Laura and Mary ate all the meat off the bones. Nothing ever tasted as good as that pig's tail! And Jack got his share, too. Laura gave him the bones to crunch.

In the winter the little log house was snug against the cold. Laura and Jack curled up by the fireside while Pa told stories and played his fiddle. Outside the wind moaned. Sometimes at night a wolf howled outside the walls of the little log cabin. Laura knew wolves would eat little girls. But she could look out from her bed and see Jack pacing back and forth in front of the door. The hair stood up along his back and he showed his sharp teeth. Pa had promised her that Jack would never let the wolves get in. Laura snuggled under the covers next to Mary, feeling safe and cozy.

One day, when spring was just around the corner, Pa made an announcement.

"I've decided to go see the West," he said. "I've had an offer for this place. We can sell it for enough to give us a start in the new country."

"Oh, Charles, must we go now?" Ma asked. The weather was so cold and the house so cozy.

"If we are going this year, we must go now," Pa said. "We can't cross the Mississippi after the ice breaks."

So Pa sold the little house. He sold the cow and the calf. He stretched a white canvas cover over the wagon. Soon everything was packed in the wagon and the little house stood empty.

Early in the morning the family climbed into the wagon. Laura wore her warmest clothes and her rabbit-skin hood. She and Mary held tight to their rag dolls while all their aunts and uncles and cousins kissed them good-bye. Pa picked up Mary and then Laura, and set them on the bed in the back of the wagon. Ma sat on the wagon seat next to Pa, with baby Carrie on her lap. Jack took his place under the wagon. He was going to walk all the way to the West.

At night they camped beneath the stars. And all day the wagon rolled on behind the horses. They crossed creeks and rivers. They drove through woods and strange, empty, treeless country.

One day Pa traded the tired brown horses for two black ponies. He told Laura and Mary they were called western mustangs.

"They're strong as mules and gentle as kittens," he explained. The ponies had big, gentle eyes and long manes. Laura and Mary named them Pet and Patty.

 6

Pa hitched Pet and Patty to the wagon, and they all traveled on together. They had come from the Big Woods of Wisconsin, across Minnesota, Iowa, and Missouri. And all that long way Jack had trotted under the wagon. It was a long trip for a little dog, but then Jack was not an ordinary dog.

CHAPTER 2

Jack and the River

One afternoon the wagon rolled to a stop. Laura looked out over Ma's shoulder. Ahead was a swift blue creek. They were in Kansas. They had left the Big Woods far behind them.

Pet and Patty dipped their noses to drink from the gurgling water. Jack followed them, lapping up the water with his red tongue.

"This creek's pretty high," Pa said. "But I guess we can make it all right. What do you say, Caroline?"

"Whatever you say, Charles," Ma answered.

Pet and Patty lifted their wet noses. They pricked their ears forward, looking at the creek. Then they pricked them backward to hear what Pa would say.

"I'll tie down the wagon-cover," Pa said. Laura watched him unroll the canvas sides. He tied them firmly to the wagon box. Then he pulled on the rope at the back of the wagon. The canvas drew together tightly, making a round hole that got smaller and smaller. Laura watched Pa through the hole. First she could see his whole head, then just his face, then just the tip of his nose. At last the hole was too small to see through at all.

Mary huddled down on the bed. She did not like fords. The rushing water scared her. But Laura was excited. She loved the sound of the water splashing against the wagon.

Pa climbed back onto the wagon seat. "The horses may have to swim a bit in the middle," he told Ma. "But we'll make it all right."

Laura thought about Jack. "I wish Jack could ride in the wagon, Pa," she said.

Ma turned to look at her. "Jack can swim, Laura," she said. "He will be all right."

Pa eased the horses into the creek. Water struck the sides of the wagon, lifting it high. The wagon dipped and swayed. It was a lovely feeling.

All of a sudden the noise stopped. Ma said sharply, "Lie down, girls!" Laura and Mary dropped flat on the bed. Ma leaned back from the wagon seat to pull a blanket over their heads. It was stifling underneath.

"Be still," Ma warned. "Don't move!"

Mary didn't move a muscle, but Laura couldn't help wriggling a little. She wanted to know what was happening. The noisy splashing came back, and then it died away again. It felt like the wagon was turning in the water.

She heard Pa yell, "Take the reins, Caroline!" His voice scared Laura.

Then there was a loud splash beside the lurching wagon. Laura just had to see what was going on. She sat up, scrambling free of the blanket.

Pa was in the rushing water with Pet and Patty. All Laura could see was his head bobbing next to theirs. He was holding on to Pet's bridle, talking to the horses. Laura couldn't hear what he was saying; the water was too loud.

"Lie down, Laura!" Ma said. She looked scared. Laura lay down next to Mary again. She felt cold and sick. The ride wasn't fun anymore.

She squeezed her eyes shut, but she could still see the water raging around Pa's head. Her stomach felt sicker and sicker. Beside her Mary was crying without making a sound.

At last Laura felt the wagon's front

wheels grate against something hard. Pa gave a shout. They were on the other side.

Laura sat up again. She saw Pa running beside Pet and Patty at the head of the wagon. Water streamed off the horses' backs as they climbed the steep bank.

"Hi, Patty! Hi, Pet! Get up!" Pa called. "Good girls!"

Finally they reached the top of the bank. The awful water rushed on below, but they were safe. Everyone was safe—Pet and Patty, Pa and Ma, Mary and Laura, and baby Carrie.

Pa stood, panting and dripping, beside the wet horses. "Oh, Charles!" Ma said.

"There, there, Caroline," Pa said. He looked at the water. "I never saw a creek rise so fast in my life. Pet and Patty are good swimmers, but they wouldn't have made it if I hadn't helped them."

Laura knew that if Pa hadn't known what to do, they would have all drowned. The creek would have rolled them over and carried them away.

"Well," Pa said, "all's well that ends well."

"Charles, you're wet to the skin," said Ma.

And then Laura remembered. She cried out.

"Oh, where's Jack?"

They had forgotten all about him. They had left him on the other side of that terrible creek. He must have tried to swim after them, but they couldn't see him struggling in the water now.

Laura swallowed hard. She knew she was too big to cry. But there was crying inside her. Poor Jack! He had followed them all the way from Wisconsin, and now they had left him to drown.

If only they'd taken him in the wagon! He had stood on the bank and watched the wagon going away from him, as if the family didn't care about him at all. He'd never know how much they wanted him.

"I wouldn't have done this to Jack for a million dollars," Pa said. He shook his head sadly. "I'd never have let him try to swim that creek if I'd known it would rise like that."

He walked up and down the creek bank, whistling and calling. But no dripping bulldog swam out of the water.

It was no use. Jack was gone.

CHAPTER 3

Eyes in the Dark

There was nothing to do but go on. They drove uphill, out of the river bottoms. Laura looked back all the way. She knew she wouldn't see Jack again, but she wanted to.

The river bluffs gave way to High Prairie. Tall wild grass swayed around the wagon. Far away, the sun's rim rested on the edge of the earth. Purple shadows began to gather over the land.

Pa stopped the mustangs. Everyone climbed out of the wagon. It was time to make camp. The wind made a mournful

16

sound as it waved across the prairie.

Laura went to Ma. "Jack has gone to heaven, hasn't he?" she asked. "He was such a good dog."

Pa answered for Ma. "Yes, Laura," he said. "God won't leave a good dog like Jack out in the cold."

But Laura didn't feel much better. She watched Pa go about his camp chores. He didn't whistle as he usually did. Laura heard him say, "I don't know what we'll do in this wild country without a good watchdog."

Pa unhitched Pet and Patty. He put them on ropes so they could graze. Then he built a fire while Ma mixed up some corn cakes and fried slices of salt pork. Soon the family gathered near the fire to eat supper off their tin plates.

While they were eating, the purple

shadows closed around the camp fire. The vast prairie was dark and still. Laura and Mary began to get sleepy.

Ma was washing the dishes when a long, wailing howl rose up in the darkness. They all knew what that meant.

"Wolves," Pa said. "Half a mile away, I'd judge. I wish . . ."

He didn't say what he wished, but Laura knew. He wished that Jack were there. When wolves had howled in the Big Woods, Laura had always known that Jack wouldn't let them hurt her. A lump came into her throat and her eyes stung.

The wolf howled again. Laura jumped up and stared into the night. She saw something!

Two green lights were shining in the darkness beyond the fire. Two green lights close to the ground. They were eyes.

A cold chill ran up Laura's backbone. The green lights moved closer.

"Look, Pa!" Laura cried. "A wolf!"

In an instant Pa had his gun out, ready to fire at those green eyes. The eyes stopped moving. They stared at Pa in the darkness.

"It can't be a wolf," Pa said. "Unless it's a mad wolf. And it's not that." He pointed to the horses. They were still biting off bits of grass. If it had been a wolf, they'd have been nervous and fidgety.

"A lynx?" said Ma.

"Or a coyote?" Pa picked up a stick of wood. He shouted and threw the stick. The green eyes moved close to the ground, as if the animal crouched to spring. Pa held the gun ready.

The animal didn't move.

Pa began to walk toward the eyes, very

slowly. And slowly the eyes crawled toward him. Laura could see the animal now in the gray light beyond the fire. It was brown, with dark streaks.

Pa gave a shout and Laura screamed. The next thing she knew she was hugging a jumping, panting, wriggling Jack! He licked her face and hands all over. She couldn't hold him; he leaped from her to Pa to Ma and back to her again.

 20

"Well, I'm beat!" said Pa.

Jack was very tired. He gave a long sigh and sank down next to Laura. Ma gave him a corn cake, but he was too tired to eat it. He just licked it and wagged his tail politely. His eyes were red, and his belly was caked with mud.

"No telling how long he kept swimming," Pa said. "I wonder how far he was carried downstream before he landed."

Poor Jack! He'd almost drowned, and then he had to track the wagon all those miles across the prairie. And when at last he reached them, Laura called him a wolf and Pa almost shot him.

"You knew we didn't mean it, didn't you, Jack?" Laura asked. Jack wagged his stumpy tail.

He knew.

CHAPTER 4

Jack and Mr. Edwards

In Kansas they found some good land with water close by. Pa built a little log house out of trees he hauled from the creek bottoms.

A neighbor named Mr. Edwards came to help Pa with the house. He was tall and thin and brown. He told Laura he was a wildcat from Tennessee. But he was very polite and always called Ma "ma'am." He wore a coonskin cap and high black boots. He could spit tobacco juice farther than

Laura thought anyone could spit. And he could hit anything he spit at, too.

When the house was finished, Mr. Edwards helped Pa build a stable for the horses. And the very next day, when Laura went to see the horses, she was amazed to find a long-legged, long-eared, wobbly little colt standing beside Pet.

Pa said it was a mule. Its ears were very long. They reminded Laura of a jack rabbit. They named the little colt Bunny.

The little house was nice and snug. There were holes cut into the walls for windows, and through them Laura could see the wide prairie. Before long, Kansas began to feel like home.

Summer passed and the weather grew colder. It was time for Pa to make a trip to town. The family needed cornmeal and other supplies.

He left early one morning before Laura and Mary were awake. He was headed for Independence, Kansas. He would be gone for four whole days.

Pa had hitched Pet and Patty to the wagon for the trip. Bunny was shut in the stable so that she wouldn't follow her mother. The trip was too long for a colt.

Laura and Mary stayed in the house with Ma. Outdoors was too large and empty to play in when Pa wasn't there. Jack was uneasy, too. He walked around the house alertly, watching for strangers.

At milking-time, as Ma was putting on her bonnet, Jack suddenly rushed out of the house. The hair on his back was bristling. Laura heard a yell and a scrambling, and a shout.

From outside the house they heard: "Call off your dog! Call off your dog!"

Ma and Mary and Laura ran out of the house. Hunched on top of the woodpile was Mr. Edwards. Logs shifted and groaned beneath him.

Jack had his paws on the woodpile. He was trying to climb up after Mr. Edwards.

"He's got me treed!" Mr. Edwards said. He backed along the top of the woodpile. Jack bared his teeth.

Ma could barely make Jack move away. His eyes were glaring red, as though he'd seen a wolf. He acted like he'd never met Mr. Edwards before.

Mr. Edwards climbed slowly to the ground. Jack watched his every move, growling softly.

"I declare," said Ma, "he seems to know that Mr. Ingalls isn't here."

"Dogs know more than most folks give them credit for," said Mr. Edwards.

He explained that Pa had stopped off at his place on his way into town that morning. Pa had asked Mr. Edwards to check on Ma and the girls every day while he was away.

Mr. Edwards was such a good neighbor that he'd come at chore time, to do the chores for Ma. But Jack had made up his mind not to let anyone go near the stable while Pa was gone. Ma had to shut him in the house while Mr. Edwards did the chores.

As he left, Mr. Edwards called out to Ma, "Keep that dog in the house tonight and you'll be safe enough."

The darkness crept slowly around the house. The wind cried and owls answered it with mournful calls. A wolf howled. Jack growled low in his throat.

Mary and Laura sat close to Ma in the

firelight. They knew they were safe in the house because Jack was there.

The next day was empty like the first. Jack spent the whole day pacing from the stable to the house and back. He wouldn't play with Laura at all. He was working, guarding his people.

Mr. Edwards came again to do the chores. And again Jack treed him on the woodpile. Ma had to drag him off.

"I can't think what's gotten into that dog," she said. "Maybe it's the wind."

The wind had a strange, wild howl in it. It tore through Laura's clothes as if they weren't there. And in the morning it was worse. It was so cold that Ma kept the door shut.

Mary and Laura stayed by the fire all day. They knew that Pa would have left Independence by now. That night he would have to camp on the prairie, alone with the horses and the cold wind.

The fourth day was very long. In the afternoon they began to watch the creek road through the window. Pa would be coming home soon.

Jack was watching, too. He whined to go outside. He walked all around the stable and the house. Sometimes he looked toward the creek bottoms and bared his teeth. The wind almost blew him off his feet.

When he came in, he wouldn't lie down. He paced about. The hair rose on his neck, flattened, and rose again.

He tried to look out of the window. When he whined at the door, Ma opened it for him. He trotted back to the stable to check on Bunny.

At chore-time Pa still wasn't home. Ma

brought Jack inside. She didn't want him to tree Mr. Edwards again.

When Mr. Edwards had finished the chores, he came to the house. He was stiff with cold. He offered to spend the night in the stable if Pa didn't come home. But Ma thanked him and said they'd be quite safe with Jack.

"I'm expecting Mr. Ingalls any minute now," she said.

Mr. Edwards put on his coat and mittens. "I don't guess anything will bother you, anyway," he said.

Suppertime came and went. Still there was no sign of Pa. Laura and Mary put on their nightgowns, but they didn't go to bed. Ma said they could stay up till Pa came home.

Jack stationed himself in front of the door. He paced up and down, and every now and then he growled. He would not rest until Pa walked through the door.

Laura and Mary yawned on their bench. Laura sat with her eyes very wide open. She was as determined as Jack. She'd stay up till Pa returned. But things began to sway before her eyes. Sometimes she saw two Marys, and sometimes she couldn't see anything at all.

Suddenly she heard a fearful crash. Ma picked her up. Laura had fallen off the bench, smack on the floor.

She tried to tell Ma she wasn't sleepy enough to go to bed. But in the middle of her sentence she yawned again, an enormous yawn that nearly split her head in two.

In the middle of the night she sat straight up. The wind gave a wild howl that rose and fell and rose again. Or *was* it the wind? Laura couldn't tell.

The door-latch rattled and the shutters shook. It was as if someone was trying to get in. But Jack wouldn't let anyone in, not even the wind. He rumbled low in his throat at the fierce howling.

And then Laura's eyes flew open. She had been asleep again. She looked at the fireplace, and there was Pa!

His boots were caked with frozen mud, and his nose was bright red. Laura ran to him, shouting, "Oh, Pa! Oh, Pa!"

Pa hugged her tight. He was so cold that Laura shivered in her nightgown. Pa wrapped her in one end of Ma's big shawl and Mary took the other end. Pa took them on his knees and they snuggled near the fire.

"I thought I never would get here." Pa sighed. He'd run into trouble with the wagon on his way home from Independence. Mud froze on the wheels until they wouldn't roll anymore. He had to climb out and knock the mud loose.

"And it seemed like we'd no more than started when I had to get out and do it again," he said. Then the horses had had to struggle against the wind all the way home. "Pet and Patty are so worn out, they can hardly stagger. I never saw such a wind!"

Ma brought him a steaming cup of coffee. He took a long drink and wiped his mustache clean. "Ah!" he sighed. "That hits the spot, Caroline!"

Pa showed them all the things he had bought in town. There was real glass for the windows. There was white sugar in a little paper sack. Mary and Laura each had a taste from a spoon before Ma put it away. There were nails and cornmeal, fat pork and salt, and all kinds of things.

Jack could relax now and sleep in his place by the door instead of pacing back and forth all night. He'd done his job well. Pa was home, and everyone was safe.

CHAPTER 5

Ox on the Roof

When Laura was seven years old, her family moved again. Once more they packed all their belongings into their covered wagon and set out on a long journey. This time they went to live in Minnesota. They lived in a dugout, a funny little house built into the side of a hill. The walls were dirt. The floor was dirt. The roof was grass that waved in the wind.

Laura and Mary could walk up a gently sloping path and stand right on the roof. Looking at the swaying grass, no one would ever guess it was a roof. "Anybody could walk over this house," Ma said, "and never know it's here."

Laura liked the new house. But she was sad that Pa had to give up Pet and Patty, the black ponies, and Bunny, the long-eared colt. He traded them for some oxen. Pa explained, "With those big oxen I can break up a great big field. I can have it ready for wheat next spring!"

The oxen were named Pete and Bright. Pete was a huge gray ox with short horns and gentle eyes. Bright was smaller. He had long, fierce horns and wild eyes. His coat was a bright reddish brown.

Laura looked the oxen over. Their legs were clumsy and their big hooves were split in the middle. Their noses were broad and slimy. They were nothing like Pet and Patty.

"Oh, Pa," Laura said. "I don't think I like cattle—much."

One evening Laura and Mary sat on a large gray rock out on the prairie. They were waiting for Pete and Bright to come home. Pa was working for a man in town, and Pete and Bright had no work to do until Pa was finished. They spent their days with a lot of other cattle, out where the grass was long and green.

Laura and Mary waited on the rock, just as they did every evening. Jack lay in the grass at their feet. He was waiting, too.

Suddenly Laura heard a great bellowing. The cattle were coming—and they were angry! When they reached the gray rock, the herd did not go by as it usually did. The cattle ran around the rock, bawling and fighting. Their eyes rolled. Their horns slashed at each other.

The air was choked with dust raised by their kicking hooves. Mary was so scared that she couldn't move. Laura was scared, too—so scared that she jumped right off the rock.

She knew she had to drive Pete and Bright into the stable. The cattle towered up in the dust.

Behind them ran Johnny Johnson. He was the boy who looked after the herd. Johnny tried to head Pete and Bright in the right direction. Trampling hooves and slashing horns were everywhere.

Jack jumped up. He ran toward the cattle, growling at their hooves. Laura ran, yelling, behind them.

Johnny waved his big stick. He managed to drive the rest of the herd away. Jack and Laura chased Bright into the stable. Pete was going in, too. Laura was not so scared now.

And then, in a flash, big Pete wheeled around. His horns hooked and his tail stood straight up. He galloped after the herd.

Laura ran in front of Pete to head him off. She waved her arms and yelled. Pete bellowed. He went thundering toward the creek bank.

Laura ran with all her might. She had to get in front of Pete again, to turn him back. But her legs were short and Pete's were long. The big ox raced ahead.

Jack came running as fast as he could. Pete ran faster and jumped longer jumps. And—*thump!* He jumped right on top of the dugout.

Laura saw one of his hind legs go down through the roof. That big ox was going to fall right on Ma and Carrie! Laura ran even faster.

Finally she was in front of Pete. Jack ran like lightning. He circled in front of the huge ox.

Pete heaved and pulled his leg out of the hole. Before he could do any more damage, Laura and Jack chased him off the roof. They chased him into the stable and Laura put up the bars that kept him inside.

Laura was shaking all over. Her legs were weak and her knees knocked against each other.

But no harm had been done. There was only a hole in the dugout roof where Pete's hoof had gone through. Ma stuffed it with some hay, and that was that.

Laura and Jack had saved the day.

CHAPTER 6

Cattle in the Hay

That wasn't the end of their adventures with the cattle. One day Pa and Ma hitched up the wagon and drove to town. They took baby Carrie with them.

Laura and Mary stayed home with Jack. They were old enough now to look after themselves.

With Ma and Pa gone, the prairie seemed big and empty. And there was nothing to be afraid of. There were no wolves here.

Besides, Jack stayed close to Laura. Jack was a responsible dog. He knew that he must take care of everything when Pa was away.

That morning Mary and Laura played by the creek. At noon they ate the corn dodgers and molasses that Ma had left for them. They drank milk out of their tin cups, then washed the cups and put them away.

Then Laura wanted to play on the big rock. But Mary wanted to stay in the dugout. She said that Laura must stay there, too.

"Ma can make me," Laura said, "but you can't."

"I can so," said Mary. "When Ma's not here, you have to do what I say because I'm older."

"You have to let me have my way because I'm littler!" Laura said.

"That's Carrie, it isn't you," Mary told

her. "If you don't do what I say, I'll tell Ma."

"I can play where I want to!" said Laura. She darted out of the dugout. Mary grabbed for her, but Laura was too quick.

She began to run up the path, but Jack was in the way. He stood stiff, looking across the creek. Laura looked, too.

"Mary!" she screeched.

The cattle were all around Pa's haystacks. Pa had worked for days cutting that hay and piling it into big stacks. And now those cattle were eating it!

They were tearing into the stacks with their horns. They gouged out huge chunks of hay and ate them. Hay flew everywhere, sliding off the stacks and spilling on the ground.

There would be nothing left to feed Pete and Bright and Spot, the cow, in the

wintertime. Without that hay they would starve.

Jack knew what to do. He ran growling down the path. Pa was not there to save the haystacks. Jack and Laura and Mary would have to do it. They had to drive those cattle away.

"Oh, we can't! We can't!" Mary said. She was scared. But Laura ran behind Jack and Mary came after her. They ran up onto the prairie.

The big, fierce cattle were very near. Their long horns tossed hay every which way. Their thick legs trampled and jostled, and they bawled with wide-open mouths.

Mary froze, but Laura was too scared to stand still. She jerked Mary along. She grabbed up a stick and ran at the cattle, yelling as loudly as she could.

Jack raced toward the cattle, growling. A big red cow swiped at him with her horns. He jumped behind her. She snorted and galloped.

All the other cattle ran jostling after her. But they didn't run away. They just ran around and around the haystacks. Jack and Laura and Mary couldn't chase them away.

The cattle tore off more and more hay. They bellowed and trampled. Hay slid off the stacks that Pa had worked so hard to make.

Panting and yelling, Laura waved her stick. The faster she ran, the faster the cattle went. Black and brown and red cows. Striped cows and spotted cows. Huge cows with awful horns. All of them wasting Pa's hay.

Some of the cattle were even trying to climb over the toppling stacks. Laura was hot and dizzy. Her braids came undone and her hair blew in her eyes. Her throat was raw from yelling.

But she kept on yelling, running, and waving her stick. She was too scared to hit one of those big horned cows with the stick. But she waved it in the air and yelled with all her might. Jack jumped and growled and barked at the cattle.

Faster and faster the hay slid down. Faster and faster the cattle trampled over it.

Laura ran around a haystack and there

was the big red cow, heading right toward her. She couldn't scream now. The huge legs and terrible horns were coming fast.

Laura gulped. She jumped at that cow and waved her stick. She waved it as hard as she could.

The cow tried to stop. But all the other cattle were coming behind her and she couldn't. She galloped closer and closer.

At the last second she swerved. Laura found her breath again. The big red cow ran away across the fields. And all the other cattle thundered after her.

Jack chased after them, farther and farther from the hay. Laura and Mary ran with him. Far into the high grasses they chased those cattle. Pa's hay was safe.

Johnny Johnson rose from the grass. He was rubbing his eyes. He had been lying asleep in a warm hollow.

"Johnny! Johnny!" Laura yelled. "Wake up and watch the cattle!"

Breathing hard, Laura and Jack and Mary turned toward home. The high grass dragged at their trembling legs.

Laura was glad she and Jack and Mary had saved the hay. Now Bright and Pete and Spot would have plenty to eat in the winter. But she was even gladder to get to the cool, quiet dugout, where they could all rest.

But there was more excitement to come, that day.

CHAPTER 7

Runaway!

All that afternoon they stayed in the dugout. The cattle did not come back to the haystacks. The sun began to sink.

Laura and Mary wished that Pa and Ma would come home. Again and again they went up the path to look for the wagon. After a while they went up to sit on the grassy roof of their house.

Jack waited beside them. The lower the sun went, the more Jack's ears pricked up. He was watching for the wagon, too.

Finally Jack turned his ears toward the prairie. First one ear, then the other. He looked up at Laura. A waggle went from his neck to his stubby tail.

The wagon was coming.

They all stood and watched it come. When Laura saw the oxen, she jumped up and down. "They're coming! They're coming!" she shouted, swinging her sunbonnet. She could see Ma and Carrie on the wagon seat.

"They're coming awful fast," Mary said.

Laura stood still. She heard the wagon rattling loudly. Pete and Bright were running very fast. Too fast. They were running away!

Bumpity-bump! The wagon came banging and bouncing nearer. Ma was huddled in a corner of the wagon box. She was hanging on tight and hugging Carrie close.

Pa raced alongside Bright. He shouted and waved the goad at Bright. He was trying to turn the ox back from the creek bank.

But he couldn't do it. The big oxen galloped nearer to the steep edge. Bright was nearly pushing Pa over the bank. They were all going to tumble over, Ma, Carrie, and the wagon. They were going to fall all the way down into the creek.

Pa gave a terrible shout. He struck Bright's head with the goad.

In a flash Jack jumped up. He leaped at Bright's nose. Laura ran screaming beside them.

Pa shouted and Jack jumped. Bright swerved. The wagon flashed by with Ma and Carrie hanging on. *Crash!* Bright hit the stable.

Suddenly everything was still.

Pa and Laura ran after the wagon. "Whoa, Bright! Whoa, Pete!" Pa said. He looked at Ma in the wagon box.

"We're all right, Charles," Ma said. Her face was gray, and she was shaking all over. But she was all right.

Pa lifted Ma and Carrie out of the wagon. Carrie clung to Ma's neck, crying.

"Oh, Caroline!" Pa said. "I thought you were going over the bank."

"I thought so, too, for a minute," Ma answered. "But I might have known you wouldn't let that happen."

Laura hugged Ma tight. "Oh, Ma! Oh, Ma!"

"There, there," said Ma. "All's well that ends well."

Jack stood, panting, beside them. His green eyes sparkled. He knew he'd helped save Ma and Carrie, and he was proud.

CHAPTER 8

The Blizzard

There came another day when Pa took Ma to town. This time they decided to walk. It was winter, and the weather was beginning to turn cold. But this day was as bright as a spring one.

"Mary and Laura are big girls now," Pa told Ma. "They can take care of Carrie."

Ma put on her brown-and-red shawl. She tied her brown hood under her chin. She smiled up at Pa. Laura thought she looked just like a bird, with her quick step and bright smile.

When Ma and Pa had gone, Laura and

Mary did their chores. Laura swept the floor. Mary cleared the table and washed the dishes. After Laura dried the dishes and put them away, they had the whole day ahead of them to play.

For a while they played school, but soon the house began to feel too empty and still. The whole house seemed to be listening for Ma.

Laura went outside. There was nothing to do. She went back in. The day grew longer and longer. Even Jack was restless. He walked up and down before the door.

He scratched at the door, asking to go outside. But when Laura opened it, he wouldn't go out. He lay down and then got back up. He walked around and around the room. Something was bothering him.

He went to Laura's feet and looked up at her. "What is it, Jack?" she asked.

He stared hard at her. He was trying to tell her something, but she did not understand. Jack gave a little howl.

"Don't, Jack!" Laura said. "You scare me."

"Is it something outdoors?" Mary wondered.

Laura ran outside, but Jack took hold of her dress with his mouth. He pulled her back inside. The air was bitter cold. Laura shut the door.

"Look," she said. "The sunshine's dark." The fine, bright day had disappeared.

"Maybe it's rain," said Mary.

Laura called her a goose. "It doesn't rain in the wintertime!"

"Well, snow then!" Mary snapped. "What's the difference?" She was angry and so was Laura.

They would have gone on arguing, but suddenly there was no sunshine at all. They ran to look through the bedroom window.

The sky was filled with dark clouds, rolling in fast. "A blizzard!" Mary said.

They knew about blizzards. Pa had told them. He had heard of some folks who were in town when a blizzard came up. They couldn't get back, and their children froze stark stiff because there wasn't enough wood in the house to keep the fire going.

Laura peered out the front window. Pa and Ma were nowhere in sight. Where were they? Surely it was time for them to come home.

Mary and Laura looked at each other through the gray air.

"The woodbox is empty," Laura whispered. She was thinking about those children in Pa's story. She started for the door.

Mary grabbed her. "You can't!" she cried. "We're supposed to stay in the house if there's a storm." She was right. Ma was very strict about that.

Laura jerked away.

"Besides," Mary went on, "Jack won't let you."

"We've got to bring in wood before the storm gets here," Laura insisted. "Hurry!"

They could hear a strange sound in the wind. It was like a faraway screaming. They put on their shawls and warm woolen mittens.

Laura was ready first. She looked at the dog. "We've got to bring in wood, Jack," she said.

Jack seemed to understand. He followed her out, staying close beside her.

The wind was colder than icicles.

Laura ran to the woodpile, with Jack at her heels. She piled up a big armful of wood and ran back to the house. Jack ran behind. Mary held the door open for her.

Then they didn't know what to do. Mary needed to help Laura bring in the wood. The storm was coming awfully fast. They couldn't open the door with their arms full of wood. But they couldn't leave the door open—the cold would come in.

Little Carrie spoke up. "I tan open the door!"

"You can't," Mary said.

"I tan, too!" said Carrie. She reached up both hands to the doorknob and turned it. She could do it!

Now Laura and Mary raced to bring in more wood. Carrie opened the door for them, then shut it behind them. Mary could carry bigger armfuls, but Laura was quicker.

Jack trotted behind Laura as she ran back and forth. Just as it began to snow, Laura and Mary had filled up the wood-box. But they didn't stop. They kept on dashing out for armfuls of wood. They piled it against the wall and around the stove. The piles grew bigger and higher.

The snow came down in a whirling blast. It stung Laura's face like grains of sand. When Carrie opened the door, it swirled into the house like a white cloud.

Bang! They banged the door. They ran to the woodpile. *Clop-clop-clop*, they stacked the wood on their arms. They ran to the door. *Bump!* it opened, and *bang!* it closed behind them. *Thumpity-thump!* they flung the wood onto the floor. And back outside they ran, panting.

They could hardly see the woodpile
now. The snow was swirling all around
them. The house was hard to see in the
white swirl. Jack was just a dark blob running beside them. But Jack knew where
he was. He wouldn't let them lose their
way.

Laura's arms ached and her chest
heaved. Words ran around and around in
her head. "Where is Pa? Where is Ma?

Hurry! Hurry!" The wind went on screeching.

The woodpile was gone. Mary took a few sticks and Laura took a few sticks and then there were no more. They ran to the door together. Laura opened it and Jack bounded in. Carrie was at the window, clapping her hands and squealing.

Laura dropped her sticks of wood. She turned just in time to see Ma and Pa burst out of the white blizzard. They ran into the house. They were covered with snow from head to foot.

Pa and Ma looked at Laura and Mary, who stood all snowy in their shawls and mittens. Mary said in a small voice, "We did go out in the storm, Ma. We forgot."

Laura looked at the floor. "We didn't want to freeze stark stiff, Pa," she said.

"Well, I'll be darned!" said Pa. "If they

didn't move the whole woodpile in. All the wood I cut to last a couple of weeks!"

There, piled up in the house, was the whole woodpile. Melted snow leaked out of it and spread in puddles. A wet path led to the door.

Then Pa's great laugh rang out. Ma's smile shone warmly on Laura and Mary. They knew they were forgiven for disobeying. They had been wise to bring in the wood, though perhaps not quite so much wood! And Jack had been there, as always, to help them find their way in the storm.

CHAPTER 9

Moving On

Life in Minnesota was hard for Laura's family. Every year Pa planted a crop of wheat, but the crops never thrived. One year a swarm of grasshoppers ate up all the wheat. Another year there was too little rain and the crops dried in the fields.

Pa decided it was time to move again. He had heard of a job far off in Dakota Territory. Once again the family got ready to move west.

Laura was a big girl now. She was excited to be traveling again. Laura was just like Pa.

She loved to see new places.

The bustle of packing began. Carrie was old enough now to help Pa load the wagon. Laura washed and ironed all the clothes. Food needed to be baked for the journey, and the canvas wagon cover had to be put back on the wagon.

Jack stood in the middle of it all, watching. Everyone was too busy to notice him, till suddenly Laura saw him standing between the house and the wagon.

She knew there was something wrong. Jack wasn't frisking about like he usually did, laughing and cocking his head. He stood still with his legs stiff. His forehead was wrinkled and his stubby tail was limp.

"Good old Jack," Laura said. But he didn't wag his tail. He looked at her sadly. "Pa," she called. "Look at Jack."

She stroked his smooth head. Jack

wasn't a young dog anymore. Years had passed since he had chased squirrels in the Big Woods of Wisconsin. His bristly hair was gray.

Jack leaned his head against Laura and sighed. All in an instant, Laura knew. Jack was too old to make the trip. He was much too tired to walk all the way to Dakota Territory under the wagon.

"Pa!" she cried out. "Jack can't walk so far! Oh, Pa, we can't leave Jack!"

Pa agreed with her. "He wouldn't hold out to walk it, that's a fact," he said. "I'll make a place for him in the wagon. How'll you like to go riding in the wagon, huh, old fellow?"

Jack wagged one polite wag. He turned his head aside. He didn't want to go, even in the wagon.

Laura knelt down and hugged him.

"Jack! We're going west! Don't you want to go west again?"

Always before he had been happy when he saw Pa putting the cover on the wagon. He had trotted under the wagon all the way from Wisconsin to Kansas and then to Minnesota. Every night while Laura slept in the wagon, Jack had been outside guarding it. Every morning he had been glad to begin a new day of traveling.

But now he just leaned against Laura and sighed. He nudged his nose under her hand so that she would pet him. Laura stroked his gray head. She could feel how tired he was.

"Good dog, Jack," Laura said. She gave him a good supper and then made his bed. He slept on an old horse blanket near the door. Laura shook the blanket out to make it more comfortable.

Jack smiled and wagged his tail. He was pleased that Laura was making his bed. She made a round nest in it and patted it to show him it was ready.

Jack stepped in and turned himself around once. He stopped to rest his stiff legs. Then he slowly turned again. Jack always turned around three times before he lay down to sleep. He had done it when he was a young dog in the Big Woods. He had

done it in the grass under the wagon at night. It was the proper thing for dogs to do.

He turned himself around the third time. With a bump and a sigh, he curled into his nest. Then he lifted his head to look at Laura.

Stroking his gray head, Laura thought about what a good dog Jack had always been. He had kept her safe from wolves and bears. He had helped her bring in the cows at night. He had played with her on the prairie and along the creek. When she went to school, he had always waited on the path for her to come home.

"Good Jack," she told him. "Good dog." He licked her hand with the tip of his tongue. Then his nose sank onto his paws. Jack sighed and closed his eyes. There was a long trip ahead, and he needed his rest.

In the morning when Pa spoke, Jack did not stir. Pa said that Jack had gone to the Happy Hunting Grounds.

Laura imagined Jack in the Happy Hunting Grounds, running gaily over a wild prairie. He would sniff the morning air and race the wind. He would spring over the short grass with his ears up and his mouth laughing, just as he used to.

"Good dogs have their reward, Laura," Pa said. And there never was a dog as good as Jack.

The original
LITTLE HOUSE
books

By Laura Ingalls Wilder

Illustrated by Garth Williams

LAURA INGALLS WILDER was born in 1867 in the log cabin described in LITTLE HOUSE IN THE BIG WOODS. As her classic Little House books tell us, she and her family traveled by covered wagon across the Midwest. She and her husband, Almanzo Wilder, made their own covered-wagon trip with their daughter, Rose, to Mansfield, Missouri. There Laura wrote her story in the Little House books and lived until she was ninety years old. For millions of readers, however, she lives forever as the little pioneer girl in the beloved Little House books.

RENÉE GRAEF received her bachelor's degree in art from the University of Wisconsin at Madison. She is the illustrator of the paper dolls and the Kirsten books in the American Girls Collection, as well as numerous titles in the new Little House publishing program. She lives in Milwaukee, Wisconsin, with her husband, Tim, and their children, Maggie and Maxfield.